TRYST IN ST. LUCIA

Angelia Vernon Menchan

Honorable MENCHAN Media L.L.C. 2022

Fatima wondered what she was doing at a resort of all places, she was safaris and rainforest: But she knew, her bestie Sandra was definitely a resort woman.

The driver pulled under the awning at Stilettos, the exclusive resort in St. Lucia. Fatima Francis stared out the window, wondering why she was there. But she allowed her best friend, Sandra Bishop from high school and forward to talk her into attending their twentieth high school reunion for what Sandra called *The Best and Brightest.* which was simply twenty Black kids who twenty years later were quite successful. Sandra was a financial guru, Fatima owned two education centers that were very successful in training young people who weren't going to college. They trained in computer and graphic design, medical and

3

trades fields and entrepreneurial courses. Even she was surprised by how well *she* had done. But she thought a five-day vacation costing over ten thousand dollars was ridiculous even with everything included. Sandra convinced her she could write the reunion off.

The driver got out to open the door and Sandra raced up to the door, grabbing Fatima out of the car, immediately brightening Fatima's mood. Sandra hugged her and kissed all over her face before stepping back and checking her out.

"You look amazing, almost forty and skin so beautiful. And that hair." Sandra said her eyes smiling. Fatima was beautiful with glowing brown skin, a huge natural and face only enhanced by the sun and *Ami Cole* lip oil.

4

She was dressed simply in a burnt orange dress that showed her toned arms and legs.

"You're the one, blonde hair suits you." She reached up to touch it knowing Sandra would move her head. Once her hair was in place, don't touch.

Sandra was fully permed and perfectly always made up with beautiful ebony skin. In high school they were known as the opposites but in the ways that mattered such as education, ambition and being there for each other they couldn't be more similar. They attended the same HBCU in Atlanta, but Fatima returned to Jacksonville to work and get a graduate degree before opening her first center. Sandra went to New York and Wall Street for ten years before moving to Miami five years earlier and starting her own firm. They spoke daily and saw each other several times a year but it had been five months.

Sandra linked her arm in Fatima's and led her inside as the workers gathered Fatima's bags.

"This is—a lot." Fatima said, looking around. There was native vegetation in huge pots and beautiful furnishings and art—it was luxury.

"Stop it, it's beautiful and worth every penny. It's owned by a St. Lucian man and African American woman. It rivals all the all-inclusive resorts everywhere. The food is sublime and the beaches beautiful. Relax and enjoy, you deserve this, Ms. Educator of the year."

Fatima relaxed a bit; she knew Sandra would settle for nothing less.

6

Besides I'm here now and it is gorgeous and there are beautiful, black people everywhere. She thought walking inside. *I need a vacation or something.*

CHAPTER ONE

After settling into a beautiful room next to Sandra's, Fatima showered and changed into a lilac-colored sundress and slides. Her flight from Jacksonville had taken her to New York before flying to St. Lucia. With seven hours of flight time and two hours of wait time she seriously wanted to go to sleep but there was a meet and greet in an hour at seven. She walked out on the balcony overlooking a blue water pool, there was a bridge you could walk out across. The flora and vegetation were beautiful and lush, and people were milling around. Though Black owned Stilettos had a nice international mix of clients. During the mini tour she was given she heard American English, French, Spanish and what sounded like Russian.

It is gorgeous. She admitted before going inside and checking herself out in the mirror. Her skin shone with health and her eyes were lined and her lips glossed. *I love me.*

Music was playing and Sandra and ten others were in the room when she arrived. Most she hadn't seen in twenty years—only her and Sandra of the twenty were true friends. Everyone quickly reintroduced themselves, congratulating each other on their successes. There were two physicians, four attorneys, a general in the Air Force and the others mostly finance people like Sandra. In short order eighteen had shown up, everyone was laughing and mingling in the beautiful room with glass walls, looking out over the ocean. Fatima sipped red wine, smiled graciously and was bored out of her mind. Sandra walked into her space, saying, "don't look

9

now but Marvin—Marvin Madison is here."
Sandra hurried away.

Fatima squared her shoulders in preparation.
She and Marvin dated two years, but she
broke up with him when she chose to go to
school in Atlanta. Marvin wanted to get
married at twenty-one and have babies, that
wasn't what Fatima wanted. She hadn't heard
from him in twenty years. He joined the army
after college as an officer and was a colonel
with sixteen years of service. He had been
married fifteen years with three children.

"Fatima." Marvin called out behind her. She
smiled and turned to face him. He was
dressed in shorts and a polo and was as
handsome ever. Marvin was just over six feet,
fit with smooth chocolate skin, sprinkles of
gray in his hair and a ready smile. She

relaxed, realizing at this point Marvin was a good memory.

"Hello Marvin, that uniform suits you." He grinned and brushed off his shoulders causing Fatima to smile, genuinely.

"And you're even more beautiful. I've kept up with your success. You've done extremely well." She did a mock bow, thanking him.

"Not bad I suppose. My mama is thrilled."

Fatima's mom Marie worked thirty-five years as a school secretary and was very proud of her only child. Her dad Wilson was also proud but lived in Washington D.C. where he retired after almost forty years of federal service at sixty-five. Her parents were never married but she was close to them both. Wilson married and divorced three times before deciding it wasn't for him.

"I know she is. She told me you didn't have time to be married so young, you had a life to live." Fatima smiled and didn't respond; she knew Marie had.

"How is your family?" She asked, changing the subject.

"Still growing. We have three sons, twelve, nine and seven. Nina is pregnant with our girl, finally."

"That's wonderful, you wanted a big family." She spoke. "Is she here?" Fatima glanced around as if she were behind them.

"No, she's very pregnant." He said, staring down at her. "Fatima, I love my wife and family but you—were my first love."

"We were sixteen to eighteen Marvin. You made the right choice."

"Did you?"

"I absolutely did. I love my life." She said emphatically and she did. She couldn't imagine it any differently.

Marvin noticed how her eyes shined and nodded. *She does love her life.*

"Then things are as they should be," Sandra rushed over and draped her arm through Fatima's.

13

"Sorry Marvin, you've had your fifteen minutes." Sandra said, leading Fatima away. Fatima bumped her shoulder in gratitude. She heard Marvin's laughter trail behind them, Sandra was never a Marvin fan.

"Thank you."

"He has a wife and several kids and looking at you like you're on the buffet." Fatima giggled with gratitude. She was glad she finally saw Marvin, but he was simply part of her history.

¥¥¥¥¥

After three hours of smiling, small talk and three glasses of wine Fatima wandered outside. The fresh scent of the salty air assaulted her senses—there was also the scent of grilled chicken. Her stomach grumbled reminding her that other than a crudité or two she hadn't eaten. It was her own fault because there was a nice spread of creole food offered.

She glanced at her watch and realized it was ten and recalled from the brochure there was a pub over the water open until midnight. Strolling to the pub she saw couples cuddled on the beach and others dancing to reggae at a pier on the water.

This is nice. I mean seriously nice and it's great to see so many Black folks of all ages. The past two years have been harsh.

"Welcome to The New Inn," a man dressed in a black suit said in perfect English with a French accent." The sound of his voice brought a smile to Fatima's face. She loved accents coming from Black people. It reminded her of how diverse we are…

"Thank you. I'm so hungry."

"Then you're at the right place." He said as he pulled out her chair and placed a sparkling linen napkin on her lap. "I'm Alexander, can I choose for you?"

"Please and thanks."

Alexander quickly filled her water glass before going to order her food. Fatima glanced around and saw two couples and an elderly gentleman eating alone. The vibe was relaxed, and she exhaled. Her phone buzzed and she knew it was Sandra.

"Yes."

"Where are you?"

"I'm at The New Inn, the pub over the ocean. I'll see you in the morning. I love you." She heard Sandra sigh but knew she would back off. Fatima needed space and took it. Sandra could engage for hours and wake up fresh.

"Love you too, party pooper. Walk on the beach at nine am, be there."

Alexander arrived with a tray that held fish, fried with the head on, a chopped salad with several vegetables and a loaf of hard bread and Irish butter. Fatima's mouth watered as she thanked him profusely. There was also ale she knew she wouldn't drink but she quickly dived into the excellent food.

After her meal Fatima thanked Alexander and decided to walk the long way to her room.

17

You could hear the ocean in the quiet. Several couples sat under the strategically placed gazebos.

"Are you okay, Ms. Francis?" Fatima started at the unexpected voice. It was deep, rich and chocolate. A man walked into her light but kept a distance. Her eyes widened a bit. He was tall, broad, dark and though unsmiling he didn't appear threatening. His eyes were deep under thick, perfect brows and his nose and lips were all things African. He was gorgeous.

"How do you know my name?" She managed to ask, her voice sounding raspy.

"You're a special guest here. I'm Edward Delore, my parents own Stilettos. I research guests and memorize names to the extent I can or wish to. You own *Another Way to*

Learn Academy." Fatima was surprised by his words.

"That's impressive. That's your job?" She asked and a smile appeared on his face.

"Not at all. I'm my folks finance guy, my interest in people drives me to do the other. This time of night I walk and unwind." His eyes were focused on her, unblinking. She couldn't look away. There was something about him, his stare

"Fascinating. My room is right over the bridge. Your place is beautiful," she said. She felt the urge to move from under his gaze. He stepped back a bit, saying, "sleep well."

She hurried away, feeling his eyes on her.

He's unnerving.

She's beautiful and this—is not her thing. Good for her.

Fatima quickly showered and got into the plush bed. Dark intense eyes filled her dreams.

CHAPTER TWO

After the walk race on the beach, ten of the group got together for brunch. Fatima, Sandra and Marvin were three of the ten. The other ten had other activities or were sleeping in. Sandra asked only three things of them, to attend the meet and greet, the banquet on the last night and one tour of the area the next day. However, she held a room that had food, drinks and activities from noon to seven each day.

Marvin held court asking everyone what they did for a living and talking about his travels and accomplishments. Fatima's eyes glazed over.

"Marvin, what does your wife do?" Sandra asked.

"She's wife and mother to our kids. She served in the military for four years but decided taking care of us was her calling." He said proudly. Sandra frowned but Fatima listened. She was always curious but never as inclined as Sandra to boldly ask.

"Interesting. Cecilia is a bonds trader who manages to raise twins and work. However, it's quite helpful that she's married to a man who thinks caretaking isn't just for his wife. And lest you think he's a slacker, he's not, he owns a successful business." Sandra said lightly. Marvin's mouth opened and closed rapidly. The Colonel wasn't used to being responded to. "And before you say I don't have a husband—just know I haven't sought out one since I was widowed." Marvin looked sheepish. He likely hadn't known Sandra was a widow.

22

Fatima held back the laughter and glanced at Cecelia Montgomery who winked at her. She seemed as amused as Fatima. Marvin was pompous.

Before Marvin could respond Edward Delore walked up to their table. He looked even better in the light of day. He was wearing dark slacks, a sparkling white shirt with leather shoes and that skin looked...like velvet. Unlike everyone else who worked there he didn't wear an identifying name tag.

"Ms. Sandra, are you and your guests enjoying yourselves?" He asked, his rich tones caressing Fatima's ears. She couldn't look away from him and his eyes held hers though he addressed Sandra.

"Edward, everything is wonderful. Your place is wonderful." Sandra replied.

"It's my parents place but I thank you on their behalf. My father was born and bred here, moving to New York to attend college. My mother is from Miami but also attended NYU where they met forty-five years ago. Both poor, smart kids with dreams and each other. This is the manifestation of them loving, dreaming and working together."

"Yes, yes." Sandra said. "I'm sure your mother worked as hard as your father." There were a few snickers around the table and a humph from Marvin.

"Ms. Francis, did you sleep well?" Edward asked and all eyes turned to Fatima.

"Umm, yes, very well, thank you." Fatima's face was flaming. She *knew* Sandra had questions.

"Wonderful. Tomorrow I will be your tour guide. We will visit the main sites, the volcano, the mud baths and the waterfalls but we will also tour the other areas off the beaten path. Bring towels, good walking shoes and swimsuits, I will provide everything else." He said before nodding and walking away. Sandra immediately turned to Fatima.

"Okay ma'am, when did you meet Edward Delore?" Sandra asked.

Fatima smiled and batted her lashes.

"On my way to bed."

"Okay, secrets. I'm not mad. That man at forty-two owns twenty percent of this and runs the money side—in addition to looking like that." Sandra said, bumping her friend's shoulder.

He's something. That's for sure. Fatima thought. She glanced up to those eyes staring at her from across the room. She stared back until someone said something. When she looked back several minutes later, he was gone.

¥¥¥¥¥

Edward chuckled to himself as he left the gathering.

Now, I've got to take them on a tour. There is something about Fatima Francis, that's making me impulsive. There was no reason to follow her last night though I convinced myself it was for her safety, though there is security everywhere. There was certainly no reason to offer to take twenty rich Black people on a tour, but I did. I must be lonely as hell.

Edward hadn't been a relationship in years. He had been too devoted to or as his last woman said, "too married to his work and his parent's dreams." He had been employed by them in some capacity since cleaning up their first small hotel as a teen. After getting his MBA at twenty-three he took over their finances as well as other private ventures he worked on. But at forty-two Stilettos kept him busiest. *I bet she gives great conversation.* He thought as he went to prep for the next day.

¥¥¥¥¥

Prior to dinner Fatima and Sandra had an hour to chat. They chose one of the gazebos and ordered drinks.

"It's not that bad is it, Fatima?"

"No, it's great. I've forced myself to not consider what could be done with the amount of money I'm lavishing on me. And I know Sandra, I deserve it or something."

Sandra rolled her eyes and grabbed her friend's hand.

"You do. Your life is devoted to giving Fatima. Enjoy this and whatever this brings. You know Edward was not our tour guide. He's feeling you…let him. He's single, you're single, you're beautiful, he's beautiful—you've got yours and he's got his. Just let it be."

"You sure read a lot into that."

28

"You know if I didn't do this money thing, I would be a gypsy reading tea leaves or something, I see things."

Sandra turned her head to look at her friend.

"I hope you see something for you Sandra. Josh has been gone five years now." Sandra had gotten married seven years ago to a great man who they discovered had leukemia after they were married. He passed five years ago, and it had been all work and travel since his passing.

"I'm not looking but I'm open to it now. That's why I'm encouraging you. We have done okay baby girl, let's make a pact to live and hopefully love." Fatima squeezed her friend's hand in agreement.

"Let's. We've come a long way baby."

They had, only daughters of single moms who encouraged them and they encouraged each other and surrounded themselves with those they could learn from, and they worked, dreamed and achieved.

¥¥¥¥¥

The group danced to reggae music on the beach sand and enjoyed a buffet of island favorites including jerk, chicken, fish and pork. Drinks flowed freely and everyone was loose. It was only seven pm but seemed later. After dancing Fatima filled a plate and sat at one of the picnic tables. Marvin who had been watching her quickly joined her.

"Marvin." She said, glancing up from her food.

30

"You are enjoying yourself."

"I am. This is wonderful. I've not taken a true vacation in two years since the pandemic. My businesses were as busy as ever during that time. I'm grateful for friends like Sandra."

"You two have always been so close. So different too."

"We are more alike than we are different, folks just see the surface of us. Sandra is loving and generous but most only see the bold glamour. She's, my sister." Sandra said before picking up a wing and biting into it. Flavors exploded on her tongue. Marvin watched her —Edward also watched her from near the bar. "This food is so good."

"I don't eat ethnic foods." Marvin said. Fatima snorted in surprise.

"Seriously, everything we ate growing up was ethnic. Please explain."

"Once I could buy my own food, I eat strictly organic meats, vegetables and fruit. No highly spiced food from questionable origins."

Fatima threw back her head and laughed. He sounded unnatural. Tears rolled down her cheeks. Marvin frowned as she laughed, Edward looked on intrigued.

"Marvin, all those greens, peas, sweet potatoes and cabbage we ate were organic. Folks grew them. Mind you they were ethnicized by adding pork for flavor but delicious and nutritious. My god man, ethnic food, who are you? What about Italian, Mexican, Korean, Greek and this—I can assure you this is great food?" Marvin's nose flared a bit at her question. His nose flaring was a tell that he was annoyed.

"I just don't. I'm particular in my tastes. I've always been."

"Do you Marvin but as for me and my taste buds, trying foods of where you are is one of life's delights." She picked up another piece of chicken and popped it in her mouth, chewing with relish. Marvin excused himself to her delight. Edward smiled from where he stood. He hadn't heard them, but body language said everything. He forced himself not to go talk to her.

There will be time for that. He thought before going to his quarters.

33

CHAPTER THREE

At seven thirty am sharp, Edward stood at the door of a van that held twenty-four—a bus really and assisted everyone as they boarded. He was wearing black shorts and a tan t-shirt. His head was covered with a hat, and he had on sunglasses. When he assisted Fatima, she noticed how good he smelled and how his large hands felt on her skin.

"Good morning Ms. Francis." He said close to her ear, sending tendrils of pleasure down her spine. She nodded, not trusting herself to speak. Once they were all boarded, he got on and stood facing them, four of the twenty were missing.

"Ms. Sandra, are the other guests coming?"

"Edward, they are hungover. You have sixteen." Sandra said.

"Excellent. Our first stop will be The Pitons, or in your words mountains. The Pitons are a remnant of a heavy volcanic eruption thousands of years ago. Like many other Caribbean islands, St. Lucia is of volcanic origin. The island is still volcanically active. We will drive through the larger mountain. But first we will see the real St. Lucia. Under your seats is a box with fruit, Jamaican bread and bottled water. We will have a meal at midday. So, relax and enjoy."

"I have a question." Marvin said. Fatima and Sandra exchanged glances.

"I'm at your disposal." Edward said.

"Wouldn't it be less expensive to have a cheaper van for excursions. A twenty-four passenger Benz is a lot."

"Stilettos offers luxury sir, luxury costs." Edward answered as he pulled into traffic. Sandra kissed her teeth.

For more than an hour he drove through different living areas. Some were beautiful and often inhabited by foreigners. In others the poverty was crushing and hard to look at.

"More than twenty percent of St. Lucian's live at or below the poverty level. It's not how many of you know poverty, it's dollars a day in income. But the spirit of my people remains strong, we work hard and assist our brothers and sisters. A dime of every dollar you spend at Stilettos goes into the community which means you all contributed almost twenty thousand dollars to education, housing and life for native St. Lucians. My father grew up poor here, but his hardworking parents and his mind took him to NYU." Edward said. "Next stop The Pitons."

It was not possible to explain how it felt driving into the volcano for Fatima. It was otherworldly and was enhanced greatly by getting fully covered in mud later and swimming in natural waterfalls. After her swim Fatima stretched out near the water.

"You love the water." Edward said. He stood over her trying not to stare too hard. Her swimsuit was a relatively modest one piece, but her body was lush, and she was very comfortable in her well cared for skin.

"I do. Water is energy. I live near the ocean at home. This Mr. Edward Delore has been divine." His eyes narrowed at how his name sounded in her mouth.

"Please call me Edward."

"Only if you call me Ms. Fatima." She saw the expression on his face and giggled. "Just kidding, I'm Fatima, Edward." She stood and stretched before grabbing her bag, everyone else had gone to change.

"Fatima, it is." He said, his voice husky. Her butt spilled out of her swimsuit and her legs were beautiful. Thick but toned and sexy. "Next stop, food." He said and hurried away. He wanted to yell, *I'll call you Ms. Fatima and anything else your heart and body desires.*

¥¥¥¥¥

Edward drove to what was clearly a home. It was up in the mountains but not close to any other house. It was all brick and square.

There was nothing lavish but inside it was cool and furnished with weather friendly, comfortable furnishings. They yard was filled with mango, coconut, banana and jackfruit trees.

"This is amazing." Fatima said once they were led to a long back porch where several people were waiting to serve them. She walked to the edge of the porch as others gathered around the table. Edward followed her.

"What's amazing Fatima?" Edward whispered. She turned to face him, inches away from her.

"All of this. This beautiful house, the view of the ocean from here, the natural vegetation—all of it. I could—live here."

"I did live here. My dad purchased this land when I was a boy and built this. My parents had me at twenty-three and they were trying to build something in America, but this was home until I started school. They wanted me to have an American education. There have been other, more beautiful homes but this is *home.* I wanted *you* to see it."

A rush of feelings filled Fatima, causing her to look away.

"Let's eat." Edward said, taking her arm and leading her to a seat beside him.

Sandra looked on grinning. During the delicious creole meal Edward told them stories of St. Lucia and his grandparents who picked sugar cane as kids and later worked in the tourism industry as cooks and cleaners. Fatima drank in his words, conscience of his presence and how raptly others listened to him. He didn't talk about himself but the love of his people and homeland.

Once they were on the bus Sandra announced she was taking the night off and everyone was on their own. Right before she fell asleep on Fatima's shoulder. Fatima stared out the window at the sights around her.

"Dinner with me at ten." Edward said to Fatima as she got off the bus. It was four pm. "There is a tray of snacks in your room to tide you over until then. And nap. Ten am sharp." She didn't respond as she walked to her room. She was going and she knew he knew. Once in the room, she saw the spread but was still full of lunch. She showered and oiled and twisted her damp hair before climbing under the crisp sheets. She slept until nine.

41

¥¥¥¥¥¥

At ten pm Fatima heard a knock on her door. She sucked down the anxiety she was starting to feel. "One minute."
She stared at herself in the full mirror. Her skin was burnished from the sun and the moisturizer she used. Her dress was a simple, gold sheath in cotton. It was sleeveless and form fitting. Her shoes were dark gold sandals. She blew herself a kiss and grabbed her bag. She was surprised to see a young man at her door.

"Mr. Delore sent me to escort you for the sake of your privacy. I'm Pierre." She could only smile because a part of her anxiety was wondering how it would look. That was something her mom and Sandra often chastised her for. They both said, "Damn what they think." She followed him down a path where a small boat waited and assisted her in getting on. He sped across the water to a bungalow that sat alone from the others. Edward was at the dock waiting, dressed in white shorts and white shirt. He looked like a dark chocolate god. He assisted her from the boat, thanked Pierre and led her inside.

"Oh." She whispered.

Inside the bungalow it looked like outside. There were huge pots that held flowering fruit trees and other foliage. In the center was a round table with two huge leather chairs. The only other furnishings were two sofas and massive bookshelves. One wall looked over the ocean. He told her where the restrooms were. "This is—everything."

"It's dinner. I saw you devour the jerk and decided to cook you my version— with shrimp. The vegetables were also prepared by me, but the bread and bread pudding came from one of the restaurants." She finally turned to face him.

"Devoured Edward? Your way with words is special." He lifted his brow before walking closer.

"I love the word devour—delicious tings should be devoured." She noted the usage of tings, but his lips were making her lightheaded. She stepped back a bit and asked for a glass of water.

I need a cold shower because he made me feel devoured and he hasn't touched me.

"Fatima—your water." She took the glass from him and sipped from it. "Do you wish to eat right away or can we walk outside and talk."

"Let's talk."

He led her out to the balcony overlooking the ocean. Everything was beautiful lit by the moon and stars. There was only one seat, an oversized loveseat which meant they had to sit side by side.

"Who are you, Fatima Francis?"

"I'm a thirty-eight-year-old woman who loves what she does. I'm close to very few people, my closest are my mom, my dad and Sandra. I also love the water as you know, good books, food and to dance. Not that complicated."

Edward leaned in and sniffed her hair, causing shivers to race through her.

"I'm sure you can be and that's good. You smell edible." Fatima braced herself to not squirm at the desire building in her.

"Who are you, Edward Delore?"

"Some days outside of being Edmond and Christina Delore's son I'm not sure." His honesty tugged at Fatima's heart. "On paper I'm a finance guy with lots of education, well-traveled etc., but mostly these days I just want to be a man. I've devoted my life to work and accomplishments. I am for lack of a better way to say it, as lonely as fuck." Fatima laughed with astonishment. Edward chuckled with her.

"I didn't expect that." She finally said.

"Why not, I'm a brother ain't I?"

"You are." She murmured.

Edward leaned over and placed his lips gently on hers. Her lips and mouth opened to him in acceptance. He pressed in and explored her mouth, tongue and lips with his tongue—expertly. Moans escaped her as she returned the kisses. After several minutes she pulled away to breathe—and lick her lips.

"Did you expect that, Fatima?"

"No—but it was appreciated." She leaned forward that time, taking his face in her hands and kissing his face all over before returning to his mouth.

"Fatima—you are killing me." Edward groaned.

"Softly?" She murmured against his lips.

"So softly." He responded. "I'm going to rearrange myself and check on dinner." She watched him rush from the room. She stood and walked inside. She walked into the closet restroom and sat on the covered toilet seat.

I want him. She admitted to herself before getting up and washing up. He was placing plates on the table when she returned to the main room. There were whole fish, local vegetables and bread. There was also a bottle of champagne.

"Your kisses deserve champagne at a minimum." He said pouring them a glass. She pursed out her lips in exaggeration, drawing laughter from him. "You're funny in addition to beautiful. I know this is going to sound sexist…"

"But why am I not taken?" Her tone was dry.

"Oops."

"No oops. I know people wonder. I'm under impression there is always time for me to get taken." His eyes widened.

"Touché. Brilliant, funny and can I say sassy."

"You did. Now let me see if your cook game is tight. That's American for can this man even cook?"

"I see you Ms. Francis, with the jokes. My shrimp will give you your groove back."

49

Later, Fatima had to admit he was right. She ate two serving of shrimp, barely touching the other food. After dinner, he took her on a boat ride.

"Dinner was nice. Thank you, Edward."

"You're welcome. Who is Marvin to you?" He asked as the boat idled in the water.

"We dated in high school. He wanted to get married young but that wasn't my path. Today, he's someone I knew. He's married with kids."

"He looks like his feelings still lead him where you're concerned."

"Which means he's being led astray and how disrespectful of his wife."

50

"Facts. I'm going to escort you to your room now because—tomorrow we will have more conversation. I like you, Fatima."

"I like you."

Once they were off the boat he escorted her to her room, her arm draped through his. They passed Sandra and a few others and waved. At her room door, he kissed her gently saying, "sweet dreams."

Fatima dropped on the sofa and kicked off her shoes. In ten minutes, there was a knock. She assumed it was Sandra but was surprised to see Marvin at her door.

"Marvin, what are you doing here?"

"That's your type, some big island joker with a fancy van?" She stepped back in shock.

"Marvin, you need to get away from my door." Fatima said, her voice cold. Her fists were clenched at her sides.

"Yes Marvin, your crazy ass does." Sandra said walking between them.

"Is everything okay here?" Edward asked, walking into view. He was conversing with a guest when he saw Marvin and then Sandra headed towards Fatima's building and made his way to her room.

"Yes. Marvin is leaving. Now." Fatima said. Marvin threw up his hands and walked away.

"Fatima?" Edward said, his eyes locked on her.

"Edward, I'm good. Thanks for tonight." He walked closer and kissed her forehead before disappearing. It was one thirty am. Sandra followed her in the room.

"Marvin is a fool, but Edward honey is a man." Sandra said.

"He is and yes on Marvin. Tonight, was so good. Even with that fool coming here."

"Get some rest. We will talk tomorrow." Sandra said. She had words for Marvin. Fatima locked her door and fell on the bed fully dressed. Those kisses told promises. *Damn Marvin.*

¥¥¥¥¥

"Marvin, I'm going to return your money and ask you to leave." Sandra said. She found him at one of the bars. He turned to face her, his eyes red.

"Good. This is a bunch of bullshit anyway. A bunch of black women with a little money looking for temporary love on an island." He spat.

"If I'm not mistaken you begged for an invite to be here and check this out, temporary island love has got to be better than being married to a man chasing a woman who dropped him twenty years ago. Get your life Marvin." Sandra said, turning and walking away. Edward had been on his way to talk to Marvin, but Sandra handled it. He watched Marvin stalk away. He went to his office and reversed the charges on Marvin's account and sent him a note telling him checkout time was at eleven and his money was returned to his original account. His phone buzzed and he saw Sandra's number.

"Edward, I was going to repay him."

"Ms. Sandra, it was my pleasure. We write off stays as needed. That was needed. It's late, rest well."

Fatima, you better get him. He's a keeper. Sandra thought.

¥¥¥¥¥

Marvin slept a few hours before seeing the note on his phone. He called and ordered a taxi and made a flight reservation for later that night.

What the hell was I thinking? He asked himself but had no clear answer. Being rejected by Fatima was the one box he hadn't checked off. He wanted her to want him, even with him having a wife and kids. He remembered being told by his father, years earlier, "Jr. you cannot make a woman love or want you and if you can it won't last."

Damn all of them.

CHAPTER FOUR

It took three nights before Fatima walked outside her room into the pool that surrounded their building. It was eight am and it was just her. She slept five hours but felt refreshed. She was floating on her back with her eyes closed when she heard his voice.

"Nice." Her eyes opened slowly. She saw him on the small bridge above her. He had a cart that was filled with what looked like table linens.

"It's very nice. Are you on kitchen duty today?" She asked, swimming closer to where he stood and standing up. The pool was four feet deep and she was five nine. She was in a two-piece swimsuit and the top was a bandeau. Her breasts with huge nipples were on full display.

Damn—she's taunting me or am I tripping? Edward wondered. She was saying something with those eyes and those...

"I need to deliver this—do not leave your room, I'll bring breakfast." He said as he raced away. Smiling, Fatima swam to the room and right into the face of Sandra, who with arms folded was staring at her.

"Okay sexy, just stand up in shallow water and show that man your goods. Looking all innocent...slut. I'm so proud." Sandra said and flounced into her room.

You are going to be proud of your girl, soon. Fatima thought as she walked into her room. She quickly showered and moisturized before slipping on a Jacksonville Jaguars vintage mesh jersey. Three minutes later the door opened—Edward walked in, scooping her up in his arms. He looked down at her, his eyes conflicted.

"This might be highly inappropriate, you might sue me and win but I want—I need to get my mouth, hands on you, my dick in you…" his voice sounded harsh. Fatima slid out of his arms and pulled the jersey over her head and stood in front of him.

"Undress for me Edward." The sultriness of her tone increased his desire but slowed his movements. He took off his shirt before unbelting and sliding down his slacks and boxers. His dick sprang free, hard, heavy and thick. He walked towards her, pushing his full body into hers, pressing her on the bed. His lips found hers and explored before moving to her neck and biting into the flesh of her throat. A groan escaped Fatima as her thighs parted, her moisture wetting the bed. Edward found her nipple and tugged it with his teeth as he slid his thumb between her legs, rubbing her clit. Fatima yelled out in pleasure as he bit her flesh and rubbed her until she exploded.

"I like that, so wet and responsive. I want to get inside you." Edward murmured; his voice hoarse with desire. He looked around for his slacks to retrieve the condom. Anticipating that, Fatima reached in the drawer and handed him a condom. They came with the room. He quickly sheathed himself and started rubbing his hardness against her wetness. Fatima moved against him, giving him access, increasing their pleasure. His eyes held hers as he pushed in—hard and deep. She answered with a groan and wrapped her legs around him, pulling him in even deeper. She watched his eyes glaze from the feeling, which was so erotic, she felt another orgasm overtake her.

"Fuck, woman you're so damn sexy." He grunted, trying to hold his eruption but Fatima had other ideas as she nudged him over and took over, riding him, hard. He tried but she snatched his climax from him with her third orgasm. He wanted to beat his chest afterwards, but she was curled up on his chest.

"Fatima—

"I know Edward. I wanted this; I wanted you too." He sniffed her hair and buried his face in it.

"You honored me by allowing me to be here. I mean—you're dope as hell Fatima." She started laughing and sat up to stare down at him.

"I'm honored too Edward. You too are dope as hell." He made a face at her teasing.

"You mock me woman?" He said in heavy patois, delighting her.

"No mocking, you are dope." He grinned up at her. She loved how his eyes squinted. "You're a grown man who has handled his business in life and you're open and honest in a way I've never experienced. And your dick game is stellar." She said, holding up her fingers and kissing them with her teeth. He startled tickling her as he laughed at her antics. Fatima Francis was a deep well of beautiful personalities.

"Edward, I will pee on these sheets if you don't stop." He released her and she fled to the bathroom. Edward realized he was grinning in a way he hadn't in recent history. *And she's so damn sexy. Her sex game is stellar.*

"I hope you don't get fired." Fatima said returning to the room wearing the Stilettos robe. Edward was sitting on the side of the bed.

"I'm good—this isn't me, Fatima. I'm not out here bedding down the guests." Fatima sat down next to him.

"Edward, if I thought that I wouldn't be here—with you. There is nothing about you that indicates that, and I would know. I hope you would know in the reverse. I'm not making you my St. Lucian tryst."

"Does that mean you can stay a few extra days…get to know me, let me know you?"

The Fatima who arrived four days earlier—just four days, would have said no. But that Fatima hadn't met Edward Delore or experienced him. Or anything like him.

"My schools are on break for six weeks." Watching him she saw pleasure on his face. "But I will not stay here…no offense to you or your parents but this is not me—if had come here on vacation I would be closer to the heart of the island." Edward's eyes drank her in as she spoke. He wanted to consume her.

"Of course not. How long?"

"Let's play it by ear. I need to refocus on the events the next two days but after that I'll give you some time. You know I've checked you out, right?"

"I hope so."

He kissed her fiercely before telling her he needed to go and would see her later. Once he was gone, she climbed under the sheets that smelled like him and fell into the best sleep in years.

¥¥¥¥¥

"My goodness Fatima, stop yawning." Sandra chastised. It was their last night and Fatima had spent hours the two previous nights in Edward's arms. She needed to tell Sandra she was staying.

"I'm tired. Sandra, also I'm staying here, not here as in this place but on the island. With Edward." A snort escaped Sandra.

"I hope so. You can barely walk or stay awake. You need to stay at least until you get used to it." Fatima rolled her eyes. "All jokes aside, I hope so. Nothing but great sex, conversation and great memories may come of this but that's a good enough reason. He looks at you in a way that I've never seen and you're just as enamored. It looks amazing on you. He's the real deal Fatima."

"I know. I must stay if only for—yes, I need this. Thanks for being Team Fatima."

"Of course, it's not like I've got any other friends." That cracked them up. That's how they expressed loving each other for years.

"What happened to Marvin?" Fatima asked, glancing around the ballroom. It was the last night, and everyone was dancing, drinking and mingling. Over the course of six vacation days a lot of re-connections had been made, mostly business ones. Marvin had been the one outlier.

"He was refunded his fees and he left." Sandra said.

"I'm going to send you half of the money—I feel somehow responsible." Sandra tsked and rolled her eyes.

"Fatima, you're too much sometimes. I would have paid much more than that to get rid of his ass. He begged to come because he was an average student at best, but he's done well—He's not a general but still." Fatima snorted, Sandra could be so petty, and she loved it.

"True…"

"Besides I didn't give it to him. Edward Delore refunded it to his account. It seems there is a slush fund for getting rid of men who annoy women Edward interested in." Fatima sat up straighter.

"Really—on the refund, not all the extra."

"There is no extra, Marvin offended a guest— a special guest and poof, he's gone, money in his hand. Speaking of being gone, you better not slip out of here tonight. We *are* having breakfast in the morning." Fatima leaned over and kissed the side of her friend's face.

"I wouldn't dream of it. You are my day one."

Sandra fake frowned and pretended to wipe off the kiss, but she knew.

Fatima smiled; her heart filled. Edward had wanted to whisk her away at midnight, but she told him she had to see Sandra leave, that was their thing from always. If they weren't leaving together, they had a meal together before seeing the other off. She remembered his words.

I love that. Friends are our best thing—even more than family because we chose them. We will leave tomorrow at noon.

That pleased her because too many didn't understand or appreciate to bond of friendship—especially between women, Black women friends.

69

¥¥¥¥¥

Fatima watched the car carrying Sandra pull away from the curb, they were both blowing kisses until the car disappeared out the gate. Within seconds a beautiful black, Porsche Macan pulled up to the curve. The car stopped and Edward stepped out dressed in grey cargo shorts and a lighter grey t-shirt. There was a black baseball cap with *NYC* logo perched jauntily on his head. Fatima couldn't keep the smile off her face.

Sexy ass man.

Edward was taking her in as well in a white mini sundress, baring her shoulders, thighs and legs not to mention enhancing the body. On her feet were black and white sneakers. She held an oversized leather bag on her shoulder. Edward had retrieved her luggage the night before. Her hair was huge and free and her beautiful skin free of artifice.

Gorgeous Black woman.

He walked up close to her, looking down with a serious expression.

"Are you ready? I'm all yours for ten days or until you tire of me…" Sweet heat uncurled in her belly. She swallowed quickly but it didn't quell the excitement.

"Are you ready Mr. Delore? I don't tire easily sir." She murmured as she moved around him and walked to the car door. Chuckling, he followed her, unlocked the door and helped her inside before getting in the driver's seat and buckling up. "This car or truckette is nice!"

71

"Truckette! Okay Madame educator, I see your way with words. But it is not quite a truck. What do you drive, a hummer?"

"Not quite, I have a Range Rover. I love trucks though. This is plush." She leaned back into the headrest. "Ah…" she said as he pulled away from the resort. He worked thirty days and then usually took four or five days off but this time he was taking the ten in his contract. He told his parents he would *not* be on call. Christine had questions but he didn't answer them. Edmund applauded him.

"Whatever it is son, enjoy it." Edmund said. "You have devoted your life to us and our dreams son."

¥¥¥¥¥

Christine Delore was curious about what Edward was doing. Like her he was a workhorse and was almost always available.

"Edmund, this is very irregular. Edward never goes ghost—on us." Edmund at sixty-six, was the eider version of his son, he was a couple of inches shorter at six feet two and not as fit but the midnight skin, regal nose, full lips and hard to rattle demeanor were the same. Edward had Christine's brows and intense eyes not to mention they approached business similarly. Christine was brown skinned with well-padded curves and energy to burn at sixty-five. She easily appeared younger.

"Chris, it's past time. The man is forty-two, no wife and no children. He has no life—really. He needs a life other than this. He knows this is his legacy and he will honor that, but we chose this. Let him live." Christine paced around their home in Montego Bay, Jamaica. She became concerned by what she couldn't control. She had never controlled Edward, but he had always been available. She stopped pacing and turned to face her husband.

"You sound like he's quitting or something." Her eyes were concerned. Edmund pulled her close.

"I don't think he's quitting Christine; I don't know what he's doing but I feel going forward he might do this differently. You and I are at our third home, and he has run *our* business. He also has the best people in place to run things from wherever and technology. Christine, free him to decide his life. He's a great son, a good man and he's also lonely and *needs* someone the same way we needed each other for forty-five years. No one thought us marrying would lead to this. Trust him." Christine folded herself in her husband's arms. She did trust Edward, fully. The thing is he was better at their business than they were. She knew Edmund was right, Edward had paid his dues to them and beyond.

¥¥¥¥¥

Edward stared at Fatima who had fallen asleep less than a mile into their drive. He knew the past week had been filled with early mornings, mixing and mingling all day and two of those nights he kept her up, getting to know her and inside her. He noted her lips puffed in and out when she slept, and her lashes were long, full and real. He was parked on the driveway because he wanted her to see the full effect of his mountainside home. It was solid brick and seemed to rise out of the mountain. It was small but his oasis. There was a living area, kitchen, dining area and bathroom on the bottom floor. The top floor had a huge bedroom with bathroom and another room that was an office and workout area. Both floors looked out over the island and ocean. He owned the surrounding empty lots to maintain his privacy. That was his biggest use of his considerable wealth. Only his parents and best friend William from college and who was now his attorney visited. For dating, when he dated and entertaining, he used his residence at Stilettos.

"What is this?" Fatima asked, awe in her voice. He knew exactly how it appeared; a stone structure surrounded by native vegetation appearing to jut out of the mountain. She sat up straighter and rubbed her eyes to see better.

"Let's get out."

They did and she stood outside the car staring in wonder.

"That's my home. My oasis. I built it three years ago after purchasing the land when I was thirty. Once we drive up there, you will see it's mostly illusion and is on firm ground.

"It's so beautiful and all the trees and wild plants. Wow—sorry I fell asleep but opening my eyes to this."

"I'm glad you rested and saw it like this. It's only about twenty-two hundred square feet…"

"Compared to what…the average home in America is about sixteen these days…but you're measuring by what, baller terms?"

Laughter filled his gut and burst forth. She was so—genuine.

"I don't know but it's spacious and reclusive and I love both. Let's drive up there."

Fatima was even more impressed with the inside. The rooms were huge and sparsely furnished with furniture that was tasteful and comfortable. There were lots of vintage record albums and books on oak shelving and art from varied Black American and Caribbean artists. The walls were heavy, reinforced glass windowed that were mirrored against the intense sun with no need for window shades. She sunk down onto the thick Persian rug that covered a large section of the living area floor. She lay on her back, looking up at Edward.

"I used to love sitting and sleeping on the floor as a kid. This rug with all these books—reminds me of then." She closed her eyes and Edward stared at her, his heart pounding.

She loves my floors. That is fire for reasons I can't define. She's laying on my floor. He slid down beside her, pulling her head onto his lap. Her hair felt good in his hands.

"Thanks for trusting me and for sitting on my floors." Edward said. He was trying to hold at bay the feelings coursing through him. *I don't even know her. I know she's beautiful, sexy, educated and accomplished while loving her friend but I'm seriously thinking of running away with her or begging her to stay.*

"I trusted my gut sir which led me to trust you and floors with thick rugs are everything. My home is at the beach and have this deck I

enclosed where I practically live. On the floor is an old rug of my father's mom. It had decades of dirt in it, but my dad got it professionally cleaned when I bought my home ten years ago and I spend hours there with books, coffee or tea and nuts. I work fifty hours most weeks but on Sunday that's my spot. Just me."
He heard the joy in her voice but something wistful. He related to that.

"Would it be better if someone special were lying there with you?" He asked, their eyes connecting.

"Definitely." She answered simply. "I'm hoping..."

"Hoping what Fatima?" He asked, the energy in the room shifting.

"You will lie on my rug with me one day—soon. Like this." She said and opened her arms to him. He covered her body with his before placing his mouth on hers.

"I'll make that happen."

She opened her mouth to him and her legs, causing her dress to slide up. A little wisp of lace covered her. He slid down and removed the lace with his teeth and parted her legs before his tongue went on a full tour of her sweetness. He devoured her as she flowed under his lovemaking.

"Get inside me Edmund." She pleaded after two eruptions. He quickly removed his clothing and pushed inside her, bending her legs to her chest. He heard her gurgle with intense pleasure, and he increased his tempo and their pleasure.

81

¥¥¥¥¥

Fatima sat up and noticed rain cascading down the windows. She was lying beneath a coverlet naked. She got up, stretched, pulled on her dress and walked to the window. The view was heavenly.

"Hey…" Edward said, walking up behind her. She turned to face him. He was changed into mesh shorts and a Howard University jersey.

"Hey. I need a glass of water, shower and food in that order."
They hadn't made it past the floor. After lovemaking they both slept but Edward had woken an hour ago.

"Come on." He led her upstairs to his bedroom that was massive with a custom-made bed and more shelves of books and music. There was a dark green theme in the room which included the covers on the bed and dark jade rug. There was also a sitting area with a huge chair and table. The room smelled like him. On the bed was a peach-colored sundress from her bag.

"This is living sir." She said and followed him into the bathroom where her toiletries were placed on a plush white towel and washcloth. "Oh, I need that tub." She said and pulled her dress over her head before walking to the tub and bending over to turn on the water.

"Okay Fatima, keep showing me that and your shower will be delayed." He growled. She quickly jumped in the inch of water, allowing the tub to fill around her. "I see you. We have coconut oils here. Does that work?"

"Umm hmm, pour them in." She said and he did.

He then walked to a small fridge and pulled out a bottle of water. He filled a crystal glass and took it to her, sitting on the edge of the tub. She quickly drank it and asked for a refill.

"Edward, where is the toilet?" She asked. He pointed to a door. She jumped out of the water and raced to pee. She returned and got back in the water.

"I hadn't peed since we left the hotel four hours ago. That's some throne in there. A jet back toilet. It suits you."

"I thought so. This is my vision, this house. What are you hungry for?"

"I want steak, porterhouse and roasted vegetables. I know that's short notice so maybe tomorrow." He grinned down at her.

"Ma'am, I'm part owner of a resort with twelve restaurants. I have a lot of vegetables but no porterhouse. I'll get it delivered in an hour. I only have ribeye, no bone."

"Oh, ribeye me. I love both. I eat a huge steak weekly with lots of vegetables. That's my weakness. That and ice cream with nuts and strawberries. Oh yeah, hot wings too with the tips on. I bite and crunch bones." She said, peering at him, her head barely above the water. His dick lurched at her last words.

"Okay sexy, I got you then. I like garlic and hot peppers with my steak and the veggies are purple carrots, black potatoes, broccoli and a few local veggies. I've also got ice cream and berries."

"Serve me then."

Serving you is my honor. He thought as he bowed and left to prepare food.

"That was so delicious." Fatima said popping the last bite of her twelve-ounce medium steak in her mouth. Edward mastered seasoning and grilling. "You're a chef—of course you are." Edward had watched her eat the food he prepared. She ate every bite with relish.

"Thank you. My childhood was spent in kitchens. My parents first two buildings were near NYU. They were twenty-five and twenty-six and I was three. They rented to college kids and breakfast and dinner were part of the rent. Those two dilapidated buildings on prime real estate were the seed money for Stilettos, they made a killing when they sold it. My dad was purchasing property every time he could in his homeland and my mom was creating inclusive living experiences. Two years earlier the first all-inclusive had opened in Jamaica. In that early life my mom cooked the meals, and I was at her feet and later her side. Her parents were both hotel cooks. My dad's folks cleaned hotels in St. Lucia. Everything for years went into two things— building their dream and loving and educating me. For years they lived on the properties they purchased. Three years ago, Stilettos was opened after almost forty years of working, saving, buying and selling properties with no investors. It only has two hundred rooms, but it earned money from day one. I know you didn't ask all of that but I'm proud of them."

"I'm proud with you—and they give back to the island. I love it."

"They also took care of their parents until they passed and a lot of other people. People see this and think they know—they don't." Fatima listened intently. She loved stories about dreams achieved.

"Fatima, I'll always be part of this. I'm their heir but I need a break—a life that isn't just Stilettos. I'm an island boy deep in my soul but my mother's home in Miami and my early years in New York also comprise who I am. I'm not being part of another Stilettos. My dad assured me this is it but Christine Delore, even at her age is always thinking. I want to do something like you've done, educate young men here and in America to the possibilities, the opportunities."

"Ah, that's so needed and you're so—you're definitely someone they can model." She said, he looked reflective at her words.

"In business—until several days ago my personal life was a desert. Fatima, you arrived here with a bucket of fresh water. Thanks for allowing me to partake." His look was so intense she had to glance away.

"Thanks for sipping. Our journey has been similar. Everything was about my schools. Now they would flourish without me—I'm not even sure what a personal life looks like. I haven't dated—or anything since 2019, almost three years. So, we have both had desert experiences."

"And here we are."

"Here we are." She said, lifting her glass of water. She sipped before handing him the glass to sip from.

"Fatima, I want to get to know you—date you. I know we live in different places, but I can be wherever I need to be. If that's a mutual interest."

"It's a mutual interest. I can also be wherever I need and want to be. My staff is impeccable but for the next several days I want more food like this, more naps with you, conversation and that sex thing you are so damn good at."

"I want and need that too." His voice sounded foreign to his ears. He wanted it more than he could recall wanting anything.

CHAPTER FIVE

After seven days with Edward, getting to know him and exploring the island on food, by car and helicopter and almost two weeks on the island reality stepped in.

"I have a thing tonight at Stilettos. My assistant reminded me my folks are being honored tonight and I'm the host. I want you with me." Edward said. They were sitting up on his bed. Her head swiveled to stare at him.

"I'll be fine here Edward." She said, feeling anxious. *Meeting his parents?*

"I want you with me. You have three dresses in that closet with tags on them. The pearl gray one is my favorite." Her face opened in a huge smile, the anxiety subsiding—a bit.

"It is beautiful. But my hair is crazy and my brows…" he scrunched up his face as if appraising her.

"Hmm, your hair is in braids, I know it will do something fly once it's unbraided and your brows are perfect, and you know it. Now if you want hair and makeup ordered…"

"Ugh, please don't. I get my brows threaded and facials, that's it. I just get a bit anxious at soirées with unknown people." *And with your freaking parents who will likely think I'm after their millions—or even maybe billions.*

"I promise you I'm your known. And my people are cool, most of the time. Fatima, you're my woman."

"I am—your woman?"

"You are. You've met all my personalities and my inner freak—and you're still here so yes, you're my woman." Raw laughter poured out of Fatima. He was right and he had met hers, some he introduced her to.

"Okay then—you do know I'm going to have to go home—at some point."

"I do. We got this." He said, drawing her closer and kissing her softly. "You're my woman and I am your man." She started moving in his arms, getting closer to his heat.

Oh shit—Fatima has a man. She thought, seriously grinding against him. He returned grind for grind.

That's right baby, Wind and grind on your man.

¥¥¥¥¥

"Edmund, look at your son." Christine whispered, astonishment in her voice. Edmund glanced up and saw Edward walk in with Fatima on his arms. Her hair fell in thick ringlets around her shoulders, she had done light makeup with dark eyes and dark red lips. In the form fitting dress, she looked like a goddess. Edward stood next to her in a dark grey suit, looking down at her proudly. "Who is that?"

"I have no idea, but they look good. She's beautiful."

Good for you son. Edmund thought. *You look new.*

Edward led Fatima to the front table where his parents were. Her smile was on, but her insides were filled with anxiety. Edward squeezed her hand. Edmund quickly stood, followed by Christine, who was openly perusing Fatima.

"Mom, dad, this is Fatima Francis, my woman."

Edmund grinned broadly; Christine swallowed a gasp. "Fatima, these are my parents, Edmund and Christine Delore. They are responsible for all this." Edward said, waving his hand over himself. As he hoped, giggles erupted from Fatima.

"Then, Mr. and Mrs. Delore I'm delighted to meet you. He's quite something and so is Stilettos. I was here for a week." Fatima said. Edmund offered his hand, and she shook it.

"It's great to meet you." Edmund said, Christine hadn't said a word. "You were a part of the reunion, you are the school owner, now that's impressive." Edward was staring at Fatima and Christine's eyes were on him.

"Thanks sir." Fatima said and turned to Christine, offering her hand. Christine shook it and placed a smile on her face.

"How nice." Christine said and returned to her seat. Edward pulled out a chair for Fatima.

"Great. I'm going to say my little speech and we will get this party stared." Edward said. The room was filling with well-dressed people, many of whom would stroll up to greet the Delores. Edward grabbed a microphone and tapped it.

"Hello everyone and welcome to Stilettos. We are celebrating my parents tonight, not just because they own this place but because last week, they celebrated forty plus years of marriage, and they are cool people. There will be no speeches unless they make them, but the food and champagne are flowing." Edward picked up the champagne glass on the podium holding it aloft. Everyone else did the same.

"To years of lasting love and living one's dreams. No one has ever done it like my parents, Edmund and Christine Delore!" There was heavy applause, and *Our Love by Natalie Cole* came through the speakers. Edmund led Christine to the floor where they slow danced for the crowd. The second song was *Brick House by* The Commodores. Edmund stepped back a bit watching his wife with his hand on his chin. Christine kicked off her shoes and danced for her man, showing those 70s moves. Edward whooped and Fatima clapped beside them.

That's beautiful. Fatima thought. The third song was *Got to Give It Up by* Marvin Gaye. Edward grabbed Fatima's hand and danced her to the floor. She realized they had never danced, and she loved dancing. The beat entered her, and she danced. Edward felt the same beat as they danced together. Someone yelled, "turn up," in a British accent and the floor filled with dancers.

"You got moves sir." Fatima said. Edward did a bump and twist, saying, "You already know, woman." She threw back her head as he wrapped his arm around her, pulling her closer as the music slowed to a slow groove.

"Edmund, your son is smitten." Christine said. They were sitting at their table after the first three songs.

"It looks damn good on him. She's a catch Christine. Remove your feelings." Edmund said, staring at his son and Fatima.

"I suppose I must. A bit of a warning would have been nice."

"Men don't warn their mothers they are falling in love. Did you note your son said we were married forty plus years—instead of forty-one. Because he's respecting you and our history by not saying he was a year old when we got married against both our parents' wishes. Your parents saw me as an ashy island boy and to my parents you were a big city American girl. We won't do that to Edward or the beautiful Fatima who has our son smiling and dancing." Christine felt as much as heard her husband. Edmund was the rock.

"Of course, Edmund." She snapped. He leaned over and kissed her face.

¥¥¥¥¥

At the end of the bash Fatima sat with Edward and his parents. Something had switched in Christine. She was warmer and talkative, but her guard was up. Fatima understood, she was unknown and could be a gold digger after Edward's inheritance. But she wasn't and she knew Edward knew.

"Did you dream of owning a school, Fatima?" Christine asked.

"I didn't. I dreamed of being a principal or college professor but when I graduated high school most Black kids and others weren't headed to college like me. After a conversation about trade schools with my dad, a germ of an idea was born. I wanted to train kids to think, read, write, do math and work with social skills. My kids graduate knowing how to budget, save and invest. Most kids aren't going to college or university."

"Do they pay tuition?"

"No, I have sponsors and scholarships for that. The kids also must have a good work ethic from middle school and decent grades to get into my schools."

Christine nodded, impressed. Edmund openly expressed being impressed and told her he would personally offer a few annual scholarships.

"Thank you, sir. You will receive a dossier on your students and their success. We have a great success rate." She turned to Edward and smiled. He was staring at her. She leaned in a bit.

"Me too." She murmured. His eyes narrowed sexily at her words. He cleared his throat.

"Fatima is returning to Jacksonville in a few days. I'm going with her but will work remotely." Edward said, glancing at his parents. Christine swallowed her thoughts, but her expression was cool.

"Great." Edmund said. "You can work from anywhere. Fatima, we will have a private dinner on your return. My son just told us *we* must work."

"I look forward to that." Fatima said. A smile was planted on Christine's lips.

"How long will you work remotely Edward?" Christine asked.

"Until I return mom. Two years ago, I worked from Ghana for six months." The son's eyes met the mother's who quickly glanced away.

"You did. I'm simply inquiring. Enjoy Jacksonville, especially Fernandina Beach if you can. I went there as a kid a few times. There was a beautiful beach with Black businesses and inhabitants."

"It's American Beach, I have a cottage there, my home is at Amelia Island which is right next door. My second school is in Fernandina." Fatima said.

"You have a home on Amelia Island?" A tinge of something close to interest colored Christine's voice.

"I do. Several of us have bought a little bit back of what the colonizers stole." Edmund jumped up in delight, pumping his fist.
"I love it."

"We tried getting in there—years ago." Christine said. "But they had The Ritz Carlton and there was nothing for the likes of us. We wanted an upscale Bed and Breakfast for *us.* It was just as well I suppose. But—when they said we should consider Fernandina, I was livid. Amelia Island was Fernandina." Fatima felt the older woman's ire and totally understood.

"Ms. Delore, I understand that but it's true of everywhere in America, much of the world really. They took our land, and we built it up for them. But how I see it, is much like what Mr. Delore did, purchase it as you can and get other like-minded people to do likewise. An acre here, seven acres there…we have built homes, schools, etc. in those places and then teach the history. We can't change what they've done but we can do differently. We must reclaim our own." The passion in Fatima's voice held them all in sway, especially Edward. He was enjoying getting to know her, layer by layer. He glanced at his parents, Edmund was very impressed, as was Christine but there was stoic reluctance in her.

"Enough about me. Mr. Delore I would love a coffee and pastry, could you treat me?" Fatima asked, standing.

"I would be delighted." Edmund said as he stood and escorted her from the area.

"She's brilliant and beautiful." Christine said, still staring after them.

"She is mom. I like her a lot, I more than like her."

"I can see that. I simply hope she isn't your escape route." The expression on Edward's face was priceless. It was a combination of shock, disbelief and disappointment.

"Escape route mom? You can't be serious. You have paid me a lot of well-earned money because I devoted my life to your dreams, and I say yours because you know this wasn't dad. This is you—and your husband and son gave you all of us. I have invested and invested for others for two decades, I've worked here out of love. I could have escaped years ago. She's a woman who in two weeks knows *my* dreams. I'm not trying to escape this." He waved his hand around. "I'm trying, finally to have a life of my own, a woman who doesn't give a damn about this— but gives a damn about me. If that's escaping mom, then perhaps I am—before I wake up one day and this is *all* I have. And finally, how selfish, you have *always* had your lover, your love. Excuse me." He scraped back his chair and went to find his woman. Christine wanted to cry but refused to. Every word was true. She thought Edward would be long gone—in his thirties he achieved personal wealth but when he didn't, she grew used to him—

running things, being there unattached to anyone but them and the dream.

Turning the corner near *pudding and tings* he heard Fatima's laughter. He followed the sound where she sat under an umbrella with his dad. In front of her was berry bread pudding and he knew Edmund's favorite mocha, spiked with Appleton rum. He slid on the bench next to her and picked up her cup, sipping.

"Dad, are you trying to make my woman tipsy?"

Edmund's eyes twinkled.

"Nah man, I just love to hear that laughter." Edmund said "She also loves a good bread pudding. I told her my mother made the best and *pudding and tings* is in her honor. Son,

Fatima Francis is a good, good woman and you're a good, good man. I'm going to get my woman."

"You good?" Fatima asked, her eyes searching his.

"I'm the best I've ever been Fatima. Are you good?"

"I am and this pudding and mocha is everything."

"No, you're everything." He said softly, placing his forehead on hers and running his tongue over her lips. She tasted of berries, coffee and a hint of rum.

¥¥¥¥¥

"Don't run him away or make him choose Christine." Edmund said once they were in their private suite. "You won't win this one. He's in love with her—and she loves him. They just haven't admitted it in words."

"Edmund, I know that. I know." Edmund pulled her into his arms and held her tight.

CHAPTER SIX

Christine and Edmund showed up at the airport to see them off. Christine lightly hugged Fatima before hugging her son. Since the meeting at Stilettos, they hadn't spoken except about work, Edward ensured everything was in order and everyone was in place. It wasn't necessary for Christine or Edmund to work—but he knew Christine would be more of a presence in his absence. Edmund would be whatever was needed.

"You look casual son." Christine said. Edward was dressed in black sweats by Armani and black leather sneakers. His head was adorned with his favorite NY cap. Fatima was dressed in a snug black sweatsuit with sparkling white sneakers and her hair was a huge puff. She wore no makeup. Huge Africa earrings hung from her ears.

"He looks young, Black, rich and happy." Edmund added.

"Ayyyye!" Edward and Fatima said simultaneously, followed by laughter. Christine refrained from rolling her eyes.

"Thanks mom. This is my preferred attire, right out of my very own closets. I love y'all." He said, kissing his mom and hugging his dad. Fatima waved at them both with a smile. He grabbed Fatima's hand and walked inside.

"Edmund, I don't know who is smugger, you or your son."

"It's definitely me, I'm much older." He said, taking Christine by the hand.

"Whatever. And don't judge me. I *do* want him happy."

"No judgment. Let's drive fast around the island. Edward left me the keys to the Macan."

A little smile played around her lips.

"Okay."

¥¥¥¥¥

"You ordered fried chicken at the airport?" Edward asked Fatima once they were checked in. There was a food court upstairs in the tiny airport.

"Sure did." She said and bit into the drumstick. It wasn't American with breading, but the skin was crisp, and it was flavorful. "I missed fried chicken. It's a vice of almost every African American. I'll make you my specialty with garlic oil, salt and red pepper coated with flour and fried. You might fall in love…" realizing what she said, she bit into the chicken again.

"It won't be the chicken, no matter how good it tis, milady. Believe dat." Pleasure coursed through her at his words, use of words and how he looked at her.

"Want a bite?" She asked, holding up the mostly devoured drumstick. He had ordered water and coffee.

"No, I'm good."

She bit off another piece, holding it between her lips. He leaned in and snatched it and her lips inside his teeth.

"You're a savage." She murmured.

"And you're a savagess." He said before chewing and swallowing the bite of chicken. "Not bad."

"Told you." She said, grabbing the wing. She didn't share that.

¥¥¥¥¥

"What's your father like?" Edward asked once the plane was in flight. They were flying to D.C. first. She promised her dad she would stop by for a night.

"Wilson Francis is old school brother man. He spent three years in the army and worked thirty-seven at The Pentagon in varied positions. He retired as an instructor. He's been married and divorced a few times but wasn't married to my mom. I spent summers and vacations with him in D.C. and we traveled a lot, mostly in the states because he loves local culture as do I. But we went to Canada, Hawaii and to Paris when I graduated high school. He's a good one."

"Do your parents get along?"

Fatima had to stop to think. Other than her high school and college graduation days and the opening of her schools they were never in the same room together. Not since Fatima was a teen.

"They are never in the same room. When dad visits me, we don't visit mom. She has her life, and he has his. They rarely mention the other. It was a fling that produced me. But they gave me a great life together. Mom never married but she has what she calls a man friend, for years. He's widowed with two grown sons. He's five years younger. Dad always has someone," she said. "I'm their only child. Oh yeah, my dad has a beautiful home but it's in the hood…not far from Howard University."

"That's great. I see where you get your neighborhood passion from."

"I got that from both. My mom's home is a block from where she grew up. There is a lot of gentrifications, but mom and others are holding fast."

"I love it. What mom didn't tell you about Amelia Island is it's bothered her for years. Until then she hadn't heard no since she was a child. She had the college homes in New York and a small successful boutique hotel in Maryland by then and lots of capital but was told no."

"I understand her feelings but that's the old south baby, you have known how to strategize. You can't always let them know what you're planning to do. Get the land first and then reveal your plans. Owning something first makes a big difference."

"You are brilliant."

"I just pay and paid attention. I'm going to snooze." She said and snuggled closer. Within a couple of minutes, she was sleep.

Falling in love is not about the chicken no matter how good it is.

¥¥¥¥¥

Wilson Francis was as tall as Edward but leaner. Edward had imaged a shorter man in tweed. Wilson was dressed in slacks with a button down and scruffy looking boots. Edward suspected they were scruffy on purpose. He had intelligent eyes; a ready smile and his skin was dark brown. His hair and short beard were liberally sprinkled with silver. He lifted Fatima off her feet in an embrace causing her to giggle with joy.

"Put me down old man before you hurt me," Fatma said. "And meet my man, Edward Delore. Edward, this is my dad." Edward offered his hand and shook vigorously.

"It's great to meet you Mr. Francis."

"Likewise, but please call me Wilson. So—Fatty has a man." Color filled Fatima's cheeks. Wilson had called her fatty since she was a baby. Edward's face opened in a grin, *not fatty.*

"Yes dad, I am Fatima—Fa teem a."

"I know Fatty. If he's your man, he needs to know your names. Son, do I detect an accent?"

"Yes sir. I was born in St. Lucia and spoke French as a kid, but I lived in New York during the early years. My dad is St. Lucian, my mom African American."

"Ah, we are all Africa. We have reservations at Roy Boys. I know my daughter needs her infusion of fried chicken." Fatima made a face at Edward who was absorbing it. Wilson had great energy. "If she hasn't cooked hers for you make sure you try it. It's better than her grandma's."

The three of them filled up on fried chicken, pickles, biscuits and cocktails while Wilson asked about St. Lucia and Edward filled him in, never mentioning Stilettos though he said his parents were entrepreneurs there and he worked with them. Wilson didn't ask.

"You're a good man Edward. I know you two are jet lagged, full of chicken and liquor—so rest and we will talk tomorrow.

"Thank you, sir." Edward said. Fatima led Edward upstairs to where she slept when visiting her dad. It was the master bedroom, but he always gave it to her. He slept in the guest bedroom downstairs; he had since Fatima was a teen.

They showered together and got in the huge four poster bed though it was only 830pm.

"I'm sleepy." Fatima said.

"Me too—Fatty." Edward said. Fatima pinched him hard. They slept until seven.

They spent the morning and afternoon riding around with Wilson who seemed to know everyone. Fatima sat in the back, listening to them talk. Wilson was a huge trash talker, but Edward held his own. Three hours before their flight he took them to a local steak restaurant next to the airport before dropping them off at the airport.

"Thanks dad, it will be a longer visit next time." Fatima said. Wilson kissed her forehead before taking Edward's hand in his.

"Son, I trust you with her. She's my most precious." Edward bowed slightly.

"I'm honored sir. She's precious to me as well." Wilson nodded and watched them enter the airport. Fatima turned to wave.

Good for you baby girl. He loves and respects you, that's all a father can ask. Wilson thought. *He also wants to be a husband not just a lover. You deserve that.*

"Your dad is cool."

"He is. He can be quirky if he's not feeling you. About ten years ago I introduced him to a man I was seeing he was very cold. Called him the pompous African. Never made another introduction until now." Edward stopped walking, causing her to stop too.

"So, if he called me the whatever St. Lucian, you would have what?"

"Said, Dad, no he's not. He's much more than whatever, he's, my man." She said, grabbing his hand and started walking again, hard and fast. "Don't test me, Edward Delore." He grinned and winked down at her.

"Don't test me, Fatima." He growled. She winked back, they had a flight to catch.

CHAPTER SEVEN

After walking through every room in her home and introducing them to Edward they unpacked and walked out to her balcony overlooking the marsh.

"This is beautiful Fatima. You live well." They we're facing outwards; he was standing close behind her.

"Thank you. I love it here. It's remote and quiet. It's my oasis. Honestly, I almost talked myself out of, but Sandra and my dad wouldn't allow it. I'm grateful to them."

"And your mom?"

"Marie is a simple woman. All of this is nothing she concerns herself with. She's happy for everything I accomplish. My mom worked as a school secretary all her life, saving and budgeting. Her home is lovely but modest—it's one of my favorite places on earth. The fact I have a degree, career and a home is what she cares about. But sometimes I feel unworthy of it all and I go to Sandra and or dad with that because they encourage going beyond. Mom would have said, "Baby, you already have so much." I wanted this too and I could afford it." Edward turned her around in his arms, facing him.

"This is your reward for all you've done for others. On the other hand, it's beautiful you aren't feeling entitled. It's easy to fall into that trap."

"Have you?"

"Too many times to count. My mom raised me to feel entitled, but I learned on my own to work through that. For instance, I hadn't flown commercial in years but to be with you it was worth it."

I guess he wouldn't have.

"That never crossed my mind. Were you comfortable?"

"I was very comfortable. I needed that. Fatima, I need you because—you are everything real. I haven't experienced much of that in my very charmed life. I'm grateful for that but I'm more grateful for you. Seeing *me,* being with *me.* You have no idea. Once people find out about Stilettos and the other stuff, they start seeing me differently, treating me differently. But not you from day one. I've waited all my life for that kind of acceptance." She wrapped her arms around him pulling him close. She did have an idea. She had always been the smart Black girl; successful Black woman and it came with its own challenges and expectations and treatment from others. Though his kind of life was unimaginable.

"Me too Edward. I knew you were the Prince of St. Lucian hospitality, but you led with kindness and heart."

"The Prince of St. Lucian hospitality, I see you, Fatty."

"You know I'll chunk you over this balcony."

"Chunk, what's chunk?" He asked.

"That's Negroology for pick up your big ass and throw you over the balcony." Edward stared at her a few seconds before bellowing with laughter. "Chunk!"

"Are there classes in Negroology?"

"Sho is and I'm your teacher. One word per orgasm."

He licked his lip and placed his hand under her dress and pressed his thumb against her clitoris. She started moaning in the back of her throat and opened her legs wider, giving him access. He rubbed sensually and slowly until her legs shook and she gasped in relief.

"What's my word." He asked against her lips.

"Coochie master. You mastered my Coochie."

"Coochie is good."

"See, you're a quick learner Let's go shower and tings."

"I got a ting, you got the Coochie."

¥¥¥¥¥

Edward ate three pieces of Fatima's fried chicken before saying anything. They made love before showering and walking the neighborhood. When they returned, she cooked. There were other foods, but it was the chicken she bragged about. She watched him eat it, lick his fingers, eat more and take a sip of water before doing it again while ignoring her.

"It's good." He finally said.

"Good, thank you for that." Her voice sounded a bit tight. She got up and started grabbing the plates.

"Fatima, what are you doing? I need another couple of pieces." She turned to face him, stacked dishes in her hands.

"Why? It's just good, you can get good chicken anywhere."
The laughter he was holding back roared forth.

"Woman, put down those plates and come here." She did as he asked, standing between his legs. "That was the best chicken I ever had. I don't usually eat chicken breasts but those were moist and delicious and the crust with spice, delicious." His eyes danced with amusement at her antics.

"Man, I'm sensitive about my chicken. Was it good?"

"I ate three pieces; I've never had better chicken." He said grabbing her butt and pulling her closer. In my life." He said, his voice lowering.

"Are you still talking about chicken?"

"Of course, so please let me have another piece and fresh green beans since mine are mushed under your plate but first kiss me." She poked out her lips and kissed him lightly before scurrying out of his reach.

"I'm still hungry too. You had me shook." He watched her prepare a fresh plate for him and herself.

She's so damn real. She shows her feelings, admits she gets anxious and cares that her food pleases me.

"What?" She asked as she rejoined him at the table.

"I'm admiring you, you have so many layers but you're so open too. Most of us as in successful Blacks of the world tend to be more jaded and elusive by our ages. You're an anomaly."

Fatima plucked a bit of chicken skin and placed it in her mouth. She chewed as she considered his words.

"Perhaps, Sandra and others say it all the time. I simply know who I am and where I'm from. I take none of this for granted though I worked hard for it. Edward, at the end of the day it's just stuff. Also, the kids I work with keep me grounded. But we are a jaded generation. Are you jaded?"

"I can be. I've never been a kid. I always worked, in school and alongside my parents. My friends were nonexistent really until college. Everything was working on the dream. But lately I've felt out of touch with what the world is really like. So yes, but I'm open to not being jaded or entitled. It's great being here where no one knows who Edward Delore of Stilettos or of Delore Investments is. In St. Lucia, Jamaica, some parts of New York and Miami, that's all I am. Fatima, I need this, but I want you to be part of this."

His voice was deeply serious, his eyes held hers and nothing was hidden. She stared back as openly.

"I want to be—it's been a long time since more than a handful of people saw me as anything other than *the school owner*."

"We can be us together."

"We can. Now eat your chicken." Her emotions were on full. "Tomorrow you will meet my principal and see my Jacksonville campus and you will meet Marie, the woman responsible for all of this."

"I'm looking forward to it." He picked up a piece of chicken and bit into it. Watching him chew made her squirm.

"What Fatima?"

"Later Edward."

CHAPTER EIGHT

Robert Adams was the principal of the Jacksonville campus and Fatima's longest employee. He was in his late forties, divorced with a grown son and had feelings for Fatima he kept in check. He knew she was his boss, a friend and nothing more. As far as she was concerned. He was shocked when she arrived with Edward, introducing him as her man. Edward noticed the surprise before Robert could hide it.

"Robert, I'm going to show Edward the campus and you can talk to him about operations."

"Is he applying for a job?" Robert asked. His voice was a bit sharp. Fatima's glance zeroed in on him.

"Why?" She asked. Edward watched Robert stand a bit taller and his expression neutralized. Fatima's expression was inscrutable.

"No particular reason Ms. Francis other than we are closed and that usually occurs when we're open." Robert was fully focused on Fatima as he spoke which allowed Edward to watch them. She was all business but Robert not quite.

"This isn't the usual Robert. I phoned you that we were coming and here we are. Edward is with me, and I want him to hear about operations." Nothing changed in her stance or tone, but Robert *and* Edward understood. "Why don't you do that first, I'll do the tour afterwards. Edward, I'll be next door."

Robert quickly set up the video system and got things set up.

"This video shows who we are and what we do in a capsule. It's about an hour. We also have brochures with fuller explanations. The school is forward thinking and prepares kids for life. What do you do? Can I call you Edward." They had been introduced by full names.

"Of course, Robert. I'm a businessman in St. Lucia. I'm considering doing something similar. Thanks for your time." Edward said graciously and pulled out a chair in front of the screen. Robert started the video and went to gather brochures.

Edward found the video informative and exciting. It was like viewing a well-run college but for high school students. The teachers and kids interacted, and the kids worked on real time projects. He saw when they arrived everything was state of the art at the campus.

"So, what do you think?" Robert asked at the end of the video.

"What you have done is amazing. I've never seen anything quite like it."

"This is Ms. Francis' brainchild. She's changed the education game. She took what some called trade schools to another level. There are lists of kids who want to get in and educators who want to work here." Robert gushed. Edward knew it was the highest praise and not just hyperbole for a woman Robert had a crush on.

"Excellent. Thank you."

"You're welcome. We are very protective of Ms. Francis." Robert said, handing Edward a satchel of brochures. The satchel had the school's name embossed on it.

"As you should."

"Ms. Francis is in the room next door." Edward nodded and made his way to her. She was sitting at a huge desk staring out at the parking lot.

"Your school is amazing."

Fatima swirled in the chair to face him. Her smile was huge.

"Thank you. We have about an hour to tour before going to mom's. I'll show you a workshop room and the computer lab." She said getting up. He didn't move when she reached him. "Everything okay?"

"Everything is great. Fatima—I'm falling deep for you. So deep."
She stepped even closer.

"Good because I'm falling too Edward. Let's be each other's landing place." Their eyes stayed locked several minutes and neither one moved. They *knew* how quickly things were moving but they both had waited a long time.

Robert walked in and stopped in the door. He stared several minutes before clearing his throat. They turned their heads to face him.

"Ms. Francis, I have a lunch meeting, do you want me to lock up."

"Robert, thank you. You can lock this building. I'm going to show Edward the electrician workshop and computer lab. I have my pass card for those. I appreciate you." Robert smiled and nodded before leaving the room.

¥¥¥¥¥

On the drive to Marie's Edward couldn't stop raving about the school. Being there created a fire in his belly to do more. Fatima answered his rapid-fire questions until they pulled up to a red brick home with a gorgeous front yard filled with flowers and trees. There was also an old-fashioned porch with polished stone floors.

"This is home." Fatima said, leading him to the door. The door opened and, in the door, jamb was a pretty woman with long wavy hair and light brown skin, she was curvy and thick. She looked like an older Fatima with different hair and thicker body.

"Hey ugly." Fatima said. Marie laughed, grabbing her daughter in a hug. Fatima kissed all over her face.

"Mom, this is my man, Edward Delore. Edward, this beautiful lady is my mama, Marie Miller." Marie offered Edward her hand and lightly embraced him.

"Welcome Edward." She said assessing him.

"Thanks Ms. Miller. Your yard and porch are beautiful." Marie beamed; she loved compliments on her home.

"Years of work. Come in." She led them through the house to a large, open kitchen and dining area. Everything was warm and inviting. They got seated and she quickly got glasses of iced tea with mint and lemons from her backyard. The scent of delicious food permeated the air.

"Edward, you really impressed Wilson. He never calls me, but he called to tell me you were a good man for our daughter." Marie said astonishing Fatima.

"He did?" Fatima asked before Edward could respond.

"Umm hmm."

"I thank him." Edward said. "He's a nice man."

"He's Wilson." Marie said. "I'm starving so we will eat and chat. I don't know any politics or current events, but I love sports, food and gardening." Fatima lifted her brows; Marie was not given to conversation with people she just met.

"I'm hungry too ma'am, can I assist you?"

"Just wash up."

Marie served roasted chicken flavored with sage, butter and lemon with garlic potatoes and mustard greens. There was also a key lime pound cake. Edward ate two large servings and talked baseball with Marie. Fatima relaxed and watched them. Marie loved baseball and Edward was well versed. They both loved the New York Yankees.

"How long will you be here Edward?" Marie asked after dinner, and she had shown him her massive garden.

"Until…" he said.

"I like the sound of that." Marie said and embraced him before kissing her daughter and handing them two baskets of greens, green beans, lemons and strawberries.

"You and Marie hit it off." Fatima said in the car.

"We did. She's a Yankees fan, cooks great and is lovely. On the other side, I'm a Yankees fan, loves great food and loveliness."

"Smooth, aren't you?"

"Occasionally. When we went to walk the yard and garden, she told me to treat you well or else because otherwise her and Sandra would hunt me down and torture me. And then she gave me the most amazing cake." Fatima shrugged her shoulders. She knew it was true, Marie had said it, in the softest, sweetest unblinking way. She was Fatima's first and fiercest advocate.

"I'm sure she spoke softly, and you couldn't look away when she said it."

"I couldn't, I was as you say shook, but filled with respect and admiration. Robert told me you are protected by your employees."

"Marie loves her daughter and knows the sacrifices. As for Robert and several others at the school they have a vested interest."

"Robert has a man-sized crush but knows you're his boss, but his hope was still alive until you walked in with your man."

"Glad he knows. Robert is a great principal who cares about kids and the school. That's his lane. Let's go to St. Augustine. We can see the sights, walk off the food, you're game?"

"I'm game. Tell me where to go."

I want to be wherever you are Fatima.

"At the I-95 loop, head south. It's less than an hour." She said settling her eyes on him. Feeling her eyes, he turned to glance at her.

"I feel I've known you forever Edward."

"Me too Fatima. It's like the beginning of a new life."

"Pre-Us and Us."

"Yes, I like that."

They spent hours doing every touristy thing, Fatima could think of including Ripley's Believe it or Not, The Alligator Farm and Ponce de Leon Fountain of Youth. They rode the trolley and the party train before deciding to rent a room and stay over. They shopped at Target for sweats to wear the next day.

"Did you enjoy the day?" Fatima asked after they were showered and in bed eating room service.

"It was fun, serious fun." Edward said. "It reminded me of being a kid and getting a day or two with my mom's folks in Miami. They were a big, fun-loving family who went to fairs and carnivals or partied all day at home." Fatima noted the wistful tones in Edward's voice. "But around age nine my grandmother passed and that ended the visits. My mom had never liked going once she left but she loved her mom. They were poor, hardworking, loving people. Mom tried getting her mom to move but she refused so mom built her a house on the same lot in the same hood. It's empty now. I own it. After I was out of college, I tried visiting my cousins, but we all had different lives by then. I was a foreigner in more ways than one. My grandpa died the year before grandmother, both younger than sixty."

"What about your St. Lucia family?" A smile covered Edward's face.

"Every summer before we moved back permanently, I was with dad's parents. They were also hardworking folks who were very poor, but they accepted dad's generosity because that's what families do. They both lived to the late 70s. I have a few distant cousins who all work for us. We are as close as we can be. I'm not as much of a foreigner to them but the money and Stilettos is a large bridge between us."

"Even lesser success builds bridges such as that. That's probably why Sandra and I are so close, we understood the struggle and the separation. I didn't have cousins my age because mom didn't have brothers and sisters."

"Do you want babies?" Edward asked, startling Fatima. *That* was something she thought of often these days.

"I would love a child, perhaps two. I know thirty-eight is up there, but my gynecologist said I have five good years left." That tickled her and she started laughing. It helped lighten the mood. Edward watched her with a smile on his face. Tears of laughter were streaking down her face and a bit of ketchup was near the corner of her mouth. He leaned over and licked it away before sliding his tongue inside her mouth and kissing her passionately. The laughter turned to moans.

CHAPTER NINE

Edward stayed in Jacksonville four weeks initially. They were mostly alone getting to know each other and fall in love. There were a handful of visits with Marie, a visit from Wilson and one from Sandra. There was even a concert put on by a friend of Edward's from Jamaica. But the week before Fatima started school Edmund called, needing Edward for the audit.

"I have to do this." He said to Fatima. He wanted her to go with him, but she had to go to work also. They were standing in the airport.

"Of course, you do. That's your job, I'll be here when you return. I love you, Edward." She said, wrapping her arms around him.

"I love you, Fatima. I don't count in days and weeks, but this has been the best six weeks of my life—meeting you, being with you, loving you. I have decisions to make, for my future—our future. Trust me?"

"I do trust you. Hurry back."

"I will." He kissed her before walking through the pre-boarded section. She stood watching until he turned to wave. Hot tears were splashing down her face.

Edward felt gut punched as he made his way to a private hangar to board his flight to St. Lucia. He felt he was leaving *home*. Fatima had created the feeling of home for him.

¥¥¥¥¥

"Fatima, he loves you, but you knew he had to return home." Marie said. Fatima had driven there after leaving the airport. She was assisting her mom in freezing and canning the last of the summer vegetables. Anything to stay busy.

"I know that but I'm still sad and miss him— and yes after only weeks of knowing him, being with him." Marie didn't say anything for several minutes as she focused on her tasks. Finally, she stopped and washed her hands before facing her daughter.

"Fatima, I know what it's like to fall in love fast —that happened with Wilson, but he was just passing through and he didn't fall in love." Fatima listened intently. Marie rarely discussed Wilson other than to say it was a causal relationship and she got pregnant. "When I told him I was pregnant he wasn't happy, but he accepted it. After you were born, he wanted us to continue to have—relations but I didn't want that. Wilson wasn't boyfriend or husband material. Fortunately, Edward is both. Trust him."

They both mention the word trust. Fatima noticed. *I must trust him as much as I've grown to love him.*

¥¥¥¥¥

The morning after returning Edward went to the office early. Christine was there, the accounting staff and a man he knew from another resort, Lemuel Richard. He was a finance guy like Edward. Seeing Lemuel Edward started chuckling from deep in his gut. Everyone stared on but Christine.

156

"Hello Lemuel, are you here to take my job or is my mom using you as a pawn to get me in line?" Edward asked as Lemuel offered his hand. Lemuel's face colored. The other accountants looked confused.

"He is here to become part of this team Edward. You have chosen to be bi-coastal, and I need my finance team here." Christine said. Edward was still standing.

"That's perfect. The audit is a great time for new team members especially since this makes it easy for me to resign." There was a collective gasp in the room. "My plan was to try to do this for a year or so but mom you made it easy. I own twenty percent of Stilettos and St. Lucia will always be home but I've fallen in love with Fatima, and I want a family with her."

"Everyone get out." Christine said. They hurried from the room leaving them alone.

"In love? After a few weeks. Good for you. Do you know how long it took me to fall in love with your father, it took years. Because love isn't lasting but look at what is. Edward you can have any woman—many women, probably even her but to give this up." Her voice was filled with outrage. She didn't understand, her heart wasn't wired that way.

"Mom, that's because your heart is a business machine. You gave up family and everything for *this*. And dad's love and heart were enough to sustain you both. I realized years ago I was simply part of the machine. Your brilliant son who did calculations in his head and was devoted to you and only you. I love you mom, but I'm done. Where is dad?"

"Somewhere down in the town." She said and Edward heard something in her voice. Her dad was also tired though he would never be done. Stilettos was a great legacy, but the costs were immeasurable.

"Mom, I'll always be your son and available as you need me, but I want and need a life before I'm…I need it. Also, thanks for asking me to work on my vacation, otherwise I would have been in Israel when Fatima was here. As grandmother used to say in Miami, "Won't God make it work?" He kissed her lightly before calling the team in. Christine hardened her face.

They worked twelve hours until the audits were done. Only Edward, Christine and Lemuel were left.

"Lem, come through the rest of this week."
Edward said. "Be prepared to work twelve-
hour days. Mom, I'm going to find dad." It
was nine pm. Edward had popped his head in
about seven.

Edward found his dad at *pudding and tings.*
He kissed his dad's head before sitting.
Edmund had a bowl of bread pudding.

"Order food son. I know you're hungry." The
server appeared and Edward ordered
snapper and vegetables.

"Son, you are doing the right thing. Much
later than I imagined but you were waiting for
her." Edmund said. When his father spoke,
Edward listened. "Your mother needs to
control everything, and this makes her feel
she's as good as everyone, finally. Christine
spent her life escaping and earning her way

out of Liberty City. I love her as she is. Son, you will always own twenty percent of this. More importantly you owe us nothing. You devoted your life and worked harder than anyone. Go to your life—marry that pretty gul and give me grand babies." A huge love lump filled Edward's throat.

"Thanks dad. She's—I love her dad; I want babies with her. She's very paid but she's humble and loves her people. She also listens—she even cooks for me. She loves me."

"That my son was my dream for you. I was becoming concerned you were becoming Christine. But the thing is Christine has always had me and you. You should have that too; Fatima will have you. I looked her up, she's not digging your gold." Edward howled with delight. He loved how Edmund transposed worlds.

"She's not dad. She's not even aware how much gold there is. When we left, she offered to purchase my flight ticket because I was going with her."

"Go get dat gul, you heard me!"

¥¥¥¥¥

Edward spoke to Fatima everyday he was there. He didn't mention resigning from his day-to-day duties, but Edmund asked him to continue to maintain oversight of accounts reminding him *he* owned as much of Stilettos as Christine. Christine grudgingly thanked him but was still angry and—hurt. Though she wasn't inclined to admit hurt. He spent the night with them at their home before returning to Jacksonville and Fatima.

She held him tight the next morning at the airport.

"I love you mom."

"Of course, you do, I'm your mother. I love you."

For the first time in a long time tears cascaded down Christine's face. She loved no one more than Edward she just made the mistake of thinking he was as dedicated to the dream as she was. She had raised and groomed him for it, making him a partner. He was the best at it, even better than her but he had different dreams.

Edmund held his wife close, allowing her time to grieve a bit. The next day she would be Christine Delore again, Owner and Operator of the only fully Black owned and privately held resort in the world.

CHAPTER TEN

Robert knocked on Fatima's door before peeking in. Fatima looked up from her computer. It was the second Friday of school and things were calming down. She was exhausted and hadn't see Edward in almost two weeks though they talked daily and nightly. It was August 27 and he promised returning before September 1.

"Yes Robert?"

"We have someone who just showed up—will you see them?" Before Fatima could respond Edward walked in. She screamed as she jumped up from her chair and raced to him, allowing him to lift her into his arms.

"I guess you missed me." Edward said, staring into her tear shiny eyes.

"I did. I'm so glad you're here. For how long?"

"For as long as you want me—. Her eyes searched his. "I'm still an owner in Stilettos but no longer an operator. I was thinking I could ask my woman to marry me, give her a baby or two and open another school with her—Classes specializing in hospitality and finance. What you say?"

"Yes Edward, yes, yes, yes!"
Robert and a couple of the teachers watched them, thrilled for the boss. Well, the teachers were but Robert got it. When Edward started kissing her, Robert departed.

¥¥¥¥¥

Fatima stared at the ring on her finger.
Edward placed it on her finger at the office.

"This is a nice rock, fiancé." Fatima said.

"I hope so. It's like you, rare, one of a kind and beautiful." Fatima kissed the ring.

"I love. Are you and your parents good?"

"We are good. They understand it's time for my life and that life is with you. Dad is already talking grand babies." Fatima's eyes lit up.

"I'll go half on a baby but not before we say I do—I might meet a man, sleep with him a week later and bring him home with me after another week—but be his baby mama. Not Fatima." Her expression was hilarious and made Edward laugh.

"I love you, Fatima. We need to plan a wedding."

"We will—I love you. We must tell mom before dad because his meeting you first was a thing." Edward grinned and winked.

"Mama Marie already knows. She gave her blessing when I called to ask for your hand." The surprise and delight on Fatima's face made Edward glad he had. Spending time with Marie he picked up enough clues to not speak to Wilson first as was tradition. Marie raised and nurtured Fatima making her the one to first know.

"Nice and Mama Marie, I like."

"Of course, my folks know. They know I was coming to get my woman and ask you to marry me but only your mom saw the ring. You can tell Wilson and Sandra. Do you need me in on the planning or is that all you and yours. I've planned a soirée or two."

He never ceases to amaze me.

"Us, you and me. Mom is too traditional and Sandra too cutting edge, our tastes match. It will small and intimate, right?"

"That suits me. I have one thing though; we will *not* honeymoon in St. Lucia or any resort." Fatima started snapping her fingers.

"Okay then, I'm partial to Iceland."

"Word— that's a dope idea. I've never been or considered it. Let's get married and do Iceland like it's never been done." Fatima popped out of his chair, grabbed him and started dancing around the room. She led and then he led, dancing on beat to inner music.

169

¥¥¥¥¥

"That ring is fire hunty." Sandra said. Fatima FaceTime her after they spoke to Wilson. Edward was sleeping after his ten days of twelve hours and jet lag. "Love looks good on you."

"It feels better. It's been so fast."

"No, it hasn't, you and he have been waiting and preparing for each other forever and at the right time and space it happened. Only humans put timelines on love, God doesn't. I promise you if it occurs for me like that, we ain't waiting. Piss on norms, love and marry that man." Sandra's words filled Fatima's heart and spirit.

"That's why you're my damn bestie."

"For damn life and I won't be offering any suggestions because my tastes are not your tastes. Remember when you told me that at prom. I was wearing black with gemstones everywhere and tried to get you too also. You told me quick and fast and several times since—just no white please, y'all too hot for that." Their laughter filled the room. Sandra and Fatima had *always* been genuinely happy for each other and lovingly honest with each other. "Do we have a date yet?"

"Not quite but we are going to honeymoon in Iceland—my dream place."

"That's what's up Fatty. Fatty got a man, a real man." Sandra was singing and dancing in her chair.

"I love you Sandy, talk soon."

"I love you, Fatty."

Fatima hung up smiling and went to check on Edward. He was sleeping in her bed, naked.

"That's my fiancé. He's a good man who loves me and he looks like that. He feels even better." She thought staring at him from the doorway. He rolled over on his side to face her.

"Stop ogling me woman, I'm getting up. I'm starving." She watched him stand and stretch. She raced to the bed and jumped on him, taking him back to the bed.

"Damn then. You can get it, but I need to pee, bad."
She rolled off and watched him get up and rush to the bathroom. She got up and

followed him, watching him shake the pee off. He made a lascivious face.

"I wasn't trying to seduce you, I just wanted to jump on you, see how that felt. Besides, I rocked you to sleep three hours ago."

"—cause I was thinking peeing and eating in that order but I'm always willing to give you what you want and need." She took another glance at his dick before backing out the room.

"Going to cook—we need to rebuild. Put on some clothes." She yelled. Edward took a quick shower, singing off key. He realized he had never rested as much as since he met Fatima. She worked hard but rest was part of her day. She showered and sat still after her workday for at least an hour to unwind. She said it made her more productive and less stressed. For the first time in his adult life Edward was sleeping more than four or five hours. He ran and worked out daily. Fatima was urging him to join her for yoga three mornings a week.

Fatima's eyes raked over him in white cotton shorts and t-shirt, everything noticeable for her ogling.

"Looking like live porn." She muttered. He walked up behind her and bit her neck.

"It's all for you, all of it. Please tell me those smells are what I think."

"Only if you think it's oxtail curry." His stomach grumbled loudly.

"Fill up my plate, please. When did you have time to cook that?"

"I started them earlier this week and froze them. I finished while you were sleeping. I must plan meals like this unless it's the weekend. Marie taught me to cook. Now sit down and get served."

"You know I can cook and serve you."

"And you shall. Enjoy this, there will be days I'm tired, grumpy and hungry with no intention of cooking for me or you. If you had been here the first three days of school, you would have seen it. I ate saltines on the third night. It ain't cute."

"I'll know?"

"Oh yea. But it passes with rest and food and now that I've got a man, some deep loving should be added to the list." Edward pretended to write it on his hand.

"I love me a teachable moment." She said before placing a platter of food in front of him. "You've been served."

"You are lovingly goofy. Your students must love you."

"Some do. Now eat up, I want you to serve me on this very counter later, we can call that dessert."
His tongue slid through those lips making promises she knew he could keep. Fatima made a slurping sound knowing those white shorts were tenting. Edward started shoveling food in his mouth.

CHAPTER TWELVE

It seems millionaire or is it billionaire? Who knows but the very wealthy and eligible Edward Delore of St. Lucia, New York and Miami, is in Jacksonville again. Last month we saw him dancing with school owner and our own Black royalty, school owner Fatima Francis and they were winding and grinding. We chalked that up to beautiful people being in the same place. But— he's back and they are everywhere together—and she's rocking a huge rock. Huge honey and we have seen him on the island as in Amelia where she resides. They need to announce something because we fully approve—besides we haven't seen the schoolmarm on anyone's arm in—forever. Teachers need love too and he looks qualified.

Edward read the article at Fatima's request. She watched as he read it.

"It's a bit overwrought but the facts are in there. I'm cool, are you?"

"I am. I just don't want you feeling ambushed."

"Baby, we're getting married, I'm going to be here with you, people will know and talk. To most people who see me I'm just another brother—apart from being engaged to Black Royalty."

"You saw that, huh. But if you're good I'm good."

"I am. This is old news for me, I've had what I was eating, wearing, etc. in the paper. The thing is in America, tomorrow there will be another story, not like on the island, it would spin forever. I'm jaded about it."

"Will any exes pop up?" Fatima asked.

"One or two might but all they will say is I was married to work and was sexy and generous until I wasn't." Fatima frowned. "You asked Fatima. I haven't had a girlfriend in a long time. Since then, I've had sexual encounters where everyone understood thus my generosity. What about your exes, I assume they live locally?"

"The last couple of men I dated, dated do not live here. And before you I hadn't had an encounter in a very long time."

"Don't sound testy Fatima, you brought up exes and I came straight. Truth is every man you ever dated can show up and they will know I'm your man. If one of my exes appear you let them know you're my woman. I'm forty-two and in love with you, I'm not into games." Fatima nodded feeling petty but loved.

"I guess you told me."

"I did and will. I'm not playing, you're wearing my ring and I'm here—with you."

"Period."

"Period. How's the wedding planning coming, we need to think of another house, for us? You're paying for the wedding only because you insisted but our together home is on me. Tell me where and that's my next mission and a wedding date."

A whole ass man and he's mine.

"Do you like it here?"

"I do. I love it."

"I own ten acres a few miles away…"

"I'll purchase those from you, no argument Fatima. When can I see it?"

"I need to do some work, but you can drive there and check it out." She picked up her phone, adding the directions. Edward kissed her nose.

"We are doing a thing here. It's real. Understand."

"Understood." He kissed her deeper before grabbing his keys and going to check out the property.

He was stunned by the location. It was prime real estate. *She is mine, all mine. I'm glad we waited for each other.*

"What's up young'un?" Edward turned from staring over the ocean into the face of the man who changed his life. Twenty-four years earlier as an eighteen-year-old junior in college he was chosen as an intern for a six-week course taught by Malcolm Black, one of the best financial guys ever. And a legend to young, black financiers. The man had retired at forty and was doing workshops at universities around the country. Edward's eyes lit up and he quickly offered his hand, but Malcom grabbed him in an embrace.

They were the same size and height but Malcolm at sixty-eight felt like a brick wall.

"Young man, looking good. What brings you here?" Edward was still beaming.

"I met a woman, my fiancé, her name is Fatima Francis." Malcolm grinned in response.

"I see you, Jacksonville's Education Princess with St. Lucia's Finance Prince. I like that. She's a good one. This is her land, you got plans?"

Of course, Malcolm Black knew who owns what. Edward thought. He lived almost three hours away, but he knew and likely owned his own Amelia Island acreage. He hadn't seen him since the grand opening of Stilettos.

Malcolm and Cinnamon Black were special guests.

"It is. We need a bigger home—here is good. How's Lady Cinnamon?"

"She's perfect. I have questions but no time today, let's get together soon, I'll come to you. Call me." Edward's hand touched his heart.

"I would love that. I'll tell Fatima I saw you." They embraced again and Edward watched Malcolm walk to a car, waving before he got in and drove away.

Malcolm Black. I take that as a very good sign. Edward thought. Okay Florida and of course he knows my woman.

¥¥¥¥¥

Fatima was fresh out the shower, dressed in one of Edward's jerseys when the doorbell chimed. Her face was glowing from moisturizer and her hair in twists when the doorbell chimed. She thought Edward left his keys again and hurried to open the door, he was bringing seafood from The Salty Pelican, seafood pot pies and Po'boys specifically.

She was stunned when she snatched the door open and Christine Delore stood under the awning, wearing a purple suit with gray heels, her makeup perfect. Her eyes raked over Fatima who was suddenly glad she was wearing panties.

"Ms. Delore!"

"You're going to wed my son; you should call me Christine at least. Can I come in?"

"Of course." Fatima said, stepping aside. Christine stepped into the huge entryway that held beautiful African American art and a bench on either wall. The floors were polished wood and the walls pale gold. Fatima led her into the sitting room.

"The bathroom is through the doorway; I'll get you some tea. Edward should be here soon." Fatima rushed to the kitchen. Her first instinct was to change but she already saw her. When she returned with a tray with tea and lemon scones, Christine was sitting in a large, leather armchair. She accepted the tray. Fatima sat across from her.

"Your home is beautiful Fatima. Very lovely. Don't be alarmed; I'm passing through on the way to Miami. I flew into Jacksonville with a long layover so surprise." Fatima smiled graciously; surprises weren't her thing, but she was Edward's mother. "So, when are the nuptials?" Christine asked. She picked up her tea and blew it.

"We are planning. September is winding down; we will announce mid-October and marry in mid-January."

"Are you with child?" Startled laughed escaped Fatima. *Who says with child, this woman is from the bottom in Miami.* Christine stared at her a semi amused expression on her face.

"I'm not pregnant. It might seem like a rush to you, but Edward and I think the date is perfect. The wedding will be quite small, under forty people and intimate. In my mother's garden."

"That is intimate, I guess Stilettos isn't an option."

"It isn't. Several of my educators who have worked with me since my first school opened are family and I want them there."

"We could fly them—"

"I'm the bride, the expense of the wedding is mine." Fatima said firmly. Christine's brow lifted at that. She was certain Edward would pay for everything, but Fatima was full of surprises.

"How big is your family?"

"Me, my mom, dad and Sandra. Edward says it will be you and Wilson and about eight, maybe ten on his side." Christine picked up a chunk of scone and placed it in her mouth, chewing. Fatima heard Edward walk in. She remained seated.

"Hey baby." He said walking in with two large bags of food. He was focused on Fatima and didn't see Christine.

"Hello son." He stopped in his tracks at the sound of his mom's voice. He placed the bags on the coffee table and kissed Fatima before facing her.

"Mom."

"Don't get upset, I'm on the way to Miami. I stopped here. My flight is in three hours and my driver is circling the block." She stood and opened her arms for Edward's embrace. "Fatima and I had a nice visit." Edward searched Fatima's face. Her smile reassured him.

"Edward, I promise not to drop in again, but I wanted to see you—and Fatima to offer any assistance but Fatima has it all under control. You look good Edward." Fatima heard Christine's love for her son. She gathered the bags to take them to the kitchen, to give them some time.

"Mom, is everything okay? I spoke to dad, and he didn't mention you coming." Christine chewed another bite of scone.

"He thinks I flew directly to Miami. It was impulsive. It's very nice—everything is nice, and you look happy."

"Mom, I am happy. Be happy for me." She smiled but didn't reply. She hugged him again.

"I'm going to go. I just needed to see you—here. I'll be back when I'm invited. Tell Fatima, next time." He tried to walk her out, but she waved her hand. She walked outside, squared her shoulders and strolled to the car. *He's happy.*

Edward found Fatima in the kitchen, getting out bowls and silverware.

"You're good?" He asked.

"I am. Edward, be patient with her, you're her only child, son. She loves you."

"I know. Come here." She walked to him, and he held her close. "I love my mom and I must handle her. She will take over everything if given an inch." Fatima nodded, she understood. Christine had been *the* woman in Edward's life—all his life. Getting used to it being different and Fatima would take some doing.

"Malcom Black said hello."

"He's here?"

"He's gone now but is coming to visit. How do you know him?"

"He and his wife invest in my schools. They are mentors. How do *you* know him?"

"I'm a black finance guy educated in New York and D.C. and he's Malcolm Black. I interned for him in college. It changed my life.

He's the only man I have a photo of other than my dad."

"I had a huge crush on Malcolm Black until I met his wife—then my crush transferred." She stepped back and squinted at him. "Wo, y'all kind of look alike. I guess I got a type." She teased.

"I hear you Fatima but one thing I know is he only has eyes for one woman—the same way I only have eyes for you. And I'll take the look alike just don't say that around Wilson Delore. He was seriously jealous of my mentor initially. But that's all good now. It didn't help how Christine looked at the man."

"I'm sure. That man— Edward pinched her making her scream with laughter.

"Enough woman, I can be tested up to a point."

"Then what, I go over your knee?" Fatima said, dropping in a fight stance.

"If that's what you want, I got hands." He held up his large hands and desire shot through her. "That's just what I thought." He said smugly. She poked her tongue out at him.

"Yea and I'll lick it too. You already know what's in my toolbox." Fatima forgot all about cooking. She beckoned to him as she backed out of the room—he followed her.

194

EPILOGUE

The tides were high, and waves rushed in.
Edward and Fatima were sitting on ground of
the cleared off land where their home would
be created in a manner of months. It was late
October, less than three months before the
wedding and the invites were mailed and the
announcement appeared in the paper the day
before. There was also a blind item in the
newspaper.

Honeys, we are going to have a wedding. Edward
James Delore will wed the lovely Fatima Faye Francis
and we are ready. They have been doing this and that
over the past couple of months. Rumor has it the
groom to be is working on something with none other
than Malcolm Black but it's all hush, hush and on the

quiet—and the Educator of the year and bride to be is all up in it. As it should be. And sexy—fan yourselves dears because they were dancing on the square in downtown honey and they were so hot the sprinklers came on—and still they danced until steam rose— so until next honeys be excited, be very excited because when you mix St. Lucia and Jacksonville together it's got to be good.

"I'm ready for next Fatty Faye, are you?" Edward asked, his arm around his woman.

"I'm so ready Eddy James, so ready."

AFTER THE TRYST soon.

#JUSTLOVE